nickelodeon

SPONGEBOB SQUAREPANTS™

The Pet Show

story by	original art by	final color art by
Tracey West	**Vincent Deporter**	**Warner McGee**

nick.com

BENDON™

Bendon Publishing Int'l, Inc.
Ashland, OH 44805
www.bendonpub.com

It was a busy day at the Krusty Krab.
Behind the register, Squidward Tentacles
sighed. "Can I help you?" he asked the next
customer.

"May I hang up this pet show flyer?" the
fish asked. "It's for Bikini Bottom's best pet."

"Best *bet*?" asked a cheery voice. "That would be a Krabby Patty, extra cheese." SpongeBob SquarePants peeked out from the kitchen. "Want one?"

Squidward frowned. "He said *pet* not *bet*." He waved the flyer. "It's a pet show, SpongeBob NosyPants!"

"Oh, in that case, Gary's the best bet to win the pet show," SpongeBob said.

"Ha!" Squidward snorted. "More like the best bet to make the judges fall asleep. That snail of yours would *never* win."

SpongeBob rushed out from the kitchen. "How would you know? You could never have a pet as great as Gary!"

After work, SpongeBob raced home to tell Gary about the pet show. But Gary wasn't *quite* as excited as SpongeBob.

"Don't worry, Gary," said SpongeBob. "We'll prove to Squidward that you're the best pet in Bikini Bottom."

Gary gulped nervously.

The pet show was only a week away! SpongeBob got busy. He waxed Gary's shell every morning.

SpongeBob even thought up some new tricks for his pet to do.

Gary didn't like all the work, but he never complained.

Finally, the big day arrived. "We're ready!
We're ready!" SpongeBob sang.
But Gary was too tired to even meow.

Squidward had his pet hidden under a blanket. But before SpongeBob could say anything, the show began.

"I'm Fred Fishley," said the host. "Welcome to the Bikini Bottom Pet Show, sponsored by Barnacle Bites—the best food for the best pet!"

Squidward made a face. "Eww! I would never feed that slop to *my* pet," he said.

Finally, the contestants filed onto the stage.

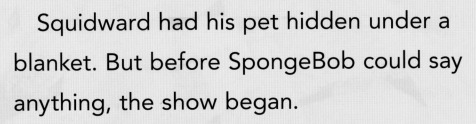

SpongeBob eyed the purple blanket in Squidward's hands. "Wow, Squidward," SpongeBob said. "I never knew you had a pet."

Squidward grinned. "And I'm sure it will beat that snail of yours." He lifted the blanket. "Behold Rocky, my pet rock!"

SpongeBob laughed.

"A rock? What kind of a pet is that?"

BA-HA-HA-HA-HA!

But the judges didn't seem to care that
Rocky was a rock. During the swimsuit
competition, the judges raved about Rocky's
seashell bikini.

Then it was Gary's turn onstage. He slid
across in a shimmering mermaid suit.

"Work it, Gary! Work it!" SpongeBob yelled.

Next it was time for
the talent contest.
"Rocky is the most
obedient pet around,"
bragged Squidward.
"Sit, Rocky! Stay,
Rocky! Play dead,
Rocky!"
Rocky just sat there.

The judges loved it.
"What a smart rock!"
they shouted.

SpongeBob started to panic. "Oh no!" he said. "The judges love Rocky. Gary, I need you to give it all you got."

"Meow?" replied Gary nervously.

"Please," SpongeBob said. "I have to prove to Squidward that you're the best pet."

So Gary did his best. He slid across a tightrope and he wrote love notes to the judges in slime.

The judges clapped and cheered.

"Great job, Gary!" SpongeBob cried. "I think you did it!"

But the contest wasn't over yet.

"It seems we have a tie for first place," said Fred Fishley. "So it all comes down to this final question: Rocky, what is the most important quality a pet can have?"

Rocky didn't make a sound.

Squidward smiled. "Everyone loves a quiet pet."

The judges applauded.

Then it was Gary's turn.

"Gary, what quality do you think makes a pet great?" Fred Fishley asked.

Gary looked at SpongeBob. "Meow," he said.

"Gary says that a pet should also be a friend," SpongeBob said. "And friends will do anything for each other. But friends also respect each other's feelings."

"Wonderful!" said the judges.

"Woo-hoo! We're going to win this
contest for sure!" SpongeBob gloated.

A sad Gary slithered off the stage.

"Gary!" SpongeBob shouted. Then he
stopped. "Wait a minute . . . ," he said
slowly. "Gary has done everything for me,
and I haven't respected his feelings at all!"

SpongeBob burst into tears. "I'm
so sorry, Gary," he said, hugging his
pet. "I don't need a contest to prove
that you're the best pet!"

Gary snuggled up to SpongeBob.
"Meow," he purred.

Onstage, Fred Fishley was about to
announce the winner. "The best pet in all of
Bikini Bottom is—"

"Just a minute!" SpongeBob interrupted.
"I'm sorry, but Gary has withdrawn from
the contest," he declared. "Come on, Gary.
Let's go home."

"Then Rocky is the winner," said Fred Fishley. "Congratulations, Mr. Squidward. You've won a lifetime supply of Barnacle Bites!"

"What," Squidward cried, "that disgusting slop?"

"Yes," said Fred Fishley, "and tomorrow your picture will be on millions and millions of cans!"

"Nooo!" Squidward wailed.

The next evening, SpongeBob prepared a special treat for Gary.

"Squidward might have won the prize," SpongeBob admitted. "But I have the best pet— and the best friend— in all of Bikini Bottom!"

"Meow!" agreed Gary.